The
Campfire Ghosts

The Campfire Ghosts

by **Susan Pearson**
illustrated by **Gioia Fiammenghi**

SIMON AND SCHUSTER BOOKS FOR YOUNG READERS
PUBLISHED BY SIMON & SCHUSTER INC.
New York • London • Toronto • Sydney • Tokyo • Singapore

For Neal Holtan,
still my favorite camper—SP

To Laura—GF

SIMON AND SCHUSTER BOOKS FOR YOUNG READERS
Simon & Schuster Building, Rockefeller Center, 1230 Avenue of the Americas, New York, New York 10020. Text copyright © 1990 by Susan Pearson. Illustrations copyright © 1990 by Gioia Fiammenghi. All rights reserved including the right of reproduction in whole or in part in any form. SIMON AND SCHUSTER BOOKS FOR YOUNG READERS is a trademark of Simon & Schuster Inc.
Designed by Lucille Chomowicz
Manufactured in the United States of America
10 9 8 7 6 5 4 3 2 1   pbk. 10 9 8 7 6 5 4 3 2 1
Library of Congress Cataloging-in-Publication Data: Pearson, Susan. The campfire ghosts. Summary: Ghosts are suspected when things start disappearing on a Thanksgiving camping trip until Ernie uses her eagle eye to find the real culprit. [1. Mystery and detective stories. 2. Camping—Fiction. 3. Thanksgiving Day—Fiction.] I. Fiammenghi, Gioia, ill. II. Title. PZ7.P323316Eah 1990 [Fic]—dc20   90-9699
ISBN 0-671-70567-9   ISBN 0-671-70571-7 (pbk.)

CONTENTS

CHAPTER 1

Martian Campers

The Martian Club was going camping. Even better, they were going on Thanksgiving. Not Thanksgiving Day, of course. But on Friday and Saturday and Sunday, they would live in the woods. They would sleep in tents. They would even cook a turkey over a campfire. Ernie could hardly wait.

It was all Daddy's idea. To celebrate their move from Newport News, Virginia, to White Bear Lake, Minnesota. Ernie was sure that no other daddy in White Bear Lake had such good ideas. She felt very proud of him. And maybe now she might even see a white bear.

Ernie skip-hopped up the street to the Martian clubhouse. On the way, she made up a song:

"A-camping we will go,
A-camping we will go,
And while we're there, we'll look for bear,
A-camping we will go."

The leaves on the ground crunched under her feet. The trees were nearly bare. But the sky was blue. The sun was almost hot. It felt like September, not November.

She skipped through Michael's side yard. The clubhouse was in the back. A sign on the door said:

> MARTIAN CLUB
> PRIVATE!
> MARTIANS ONLY!
> THIS MEANS
> PRINCE MICHAEL
> QUEEN ERNIE
> KING WILLIAM

QUEEN R.T.
EVERYONE ELSE KEEP OUT!

Another sign said:

STAR FINDER
Travel Through Space
With Commander Michael

When it wasn't the clubhouse, the play-house was Michael's spaceship.

Ernie pushed open the door. Michael was already there. He was sitting on an orange crate. His headphones were on. That meant he was listening to Mission Control. He was rubbing something with an old rag. Ernie couldn't see what it was.

"What's that?" she asked.

Michael held up a shiny gold star. It had a stickpin on its back. He stuck the pin through his collar. Then he stuck the fastener onto the pin.

"It's my space star," said Michael. "Julia cleaned out her jewelry box. She gave it to me because I'm the best space commander she knows."

Julia was Michael's big sister. Ernie thought Michael was probably the only space commander Julia knew, but she didn't say so.

Just then the door flew open. It was R.T. Her face was pink. Her thick braids were flying.

"Look what I found!" she said. She held out her hand. "A diamond ring! It was under the leaves in front of your house, Michael. I stepped right on it."

"Julia cleaned out her jewelry box yesterday," Michael explained.

"In the leaves?" said R.T. "That's a funny place to clean out a jewelry box."

Michael took a closer look. "Yup," he said. "That was Julia's, all right. She threw it out with the trash. It's not real."

R.T. slipped the ring onto her finger. "I don't care," she said. "I think it's beautiful."

"So do I," said William. He was standing

behind R.T. No one had seen him come in.

"Me too," Ernie agreed. "It's a perfect ring for a Martian queen."

"And I have a perfect star for a space commander," Michael added.

Ernie wished there had been something in Julia's jewelry box for William and her. Oh, well, camping was better than jewelry, anyway.

"Let's plan our camping trip," she said.

They pulled orange crates around the table. Michael got a pad of paper and a pencil from the shelf.

"I'll make a list of what we need," he said.

"Sleeping bags," said Ernie.

"Pillows," said Michael.

"Pajamas," said R.T.

"Warm clothes," said William. "Extra blankets."

"*Warm clothes?*" said everyone else. "*Extra blankets?*"

"It may get cold," said William. "This is very unusual weather in Minnesota, Ernie."

"Newport News weather," said Ernie.

"Indian summer," said R.T. "I think it will last one more week."

"It better," said Michael.

"Maybe," said William. He rubbed the lucky rubber rabbit he wore around his neck. "I'm bringing warm clothes, just in case."

CHAPTER 2

Chipminks and Skinks

Ernie watched the weather report every night that week. She didn't need to worry. "A record-breaking warm spell," the TV weatherforecaster kept saying. "Likely to continue through the weekend." He sounded surprised.

"Perfect weather for camping," said Daddy.

"We must have brought it with us from Newport News," said Mommy.

"Hooray for us!" said Ernie.

On Friday, Ernie and Mommy and Daddy packed the car. There were tents and sleeping bags and a backpack full of clothes and three coolers full of food. Then they picked up Michael and R.T. and William. At last they were on their way.

Ernie began to sing,

"The Martians are going camping,
The Martians are going camping,
The Martians are going camping,
To see what they will see."

Then Daddy sang a verse:

"A squirrel, a bird, a chipmink,
A bear, an owl, and maybe a skink,
The Martians are going camping—
I wonder what they'll think!"

"Chip*munk*!" cried R.T. "They may be curled up in their holes already."

"*Skunk!*" shouted Michael.

"Right you are," said Daddy. "I wonder what they'll *thunk*!" he sang.

They played the alphabet game while there were still lots of signs along the highway. When the signs disappeared, they sang.

Finally Daddy turned off the highway onto a county road. Then he turned off the county road onto a littler road. Then he turned off the littler road onto a gravel road. Then he turned off the gravel road onto a long dirt driveway.

The driveway was full of bumps and holes. Ernie and R.T. and William and Michael bounced and laughed. Mommy hung on to her door.

Then the woods got closer. The road seemed more like a tunnel than a driveway. Scruffy bushes and low branches scraped the sides of the car. The sunlight shone in patches and shadows.

"This is getting spooky," said William. He rubbed his rubber rabbit.

"Are you sure this is the right road?" said Mommy.

At last the driveway ended. Daddy stopped the car and they all got out.

In front of them was a very strange-looking house. One half of it stood tall and

straight. There were curtains in its windows. There were flowers in front of its porch. The other half was falling apart. Its shingles were flapping. Its windows were cracked. Its yard was scruffy.

"Jumping Jupiter," breathed Michael. "Are we camping in a haunted house?"

Daddy laughed. "No on both counts," he said. "We're camping in the woods on the other side of that cornfield, and the house isn't haunted. It belongs to my friend Joe. He comes here on weekends to fix it up. I guess he is only half finished."

"This is a weekend," said Michael. "Where is Joe?"

"He went to North Dakota to visit his family," said Daddy. "But he gave me a key. We can keep some of our food in his refrigerator. And we can get water from his well."

"That's all right, then," said Michael.

They carried two coolers into the house. They unloaded them into the refrigerator. Then they strapped on their backpacks.

They set off through the cornfield.

It didn't look much like a cornfield. Most of the corn had been chopped down.

"This is how Jupiter looks," said Michael.

Ernie thought he might be right, except for one corner of the field. There was still some corn standing there. The stalks were dry and brown, though.

"Joe leaves that for the birds and the hungry winter animals," said Daddy.

Sure enough, a blue jay was sitting on top of a cornstalk.

Jay jay jay! called the blue jay. He lifted off the cornstalk and flew over their heads. *Caw caw caw caw!* Then he landed on another cornstalk up ahead.

"What a racket," said Mommy. "I think he wants us to go home."

"Maybe we should," said William. He rubbed his lucky rabbit.

There was a path into the woods at the end of the field. They marched in single file. Daddy led the way. Then came William.

Then Ernie. Then Michael. Then R.T. Then Mommy. Then the blue jay. He followed them all the way to a clearing. Then he sat on a bush and scolded them some more. *Jay jay jay jay caw caw caw!*

Suddenly there was a new sound. *Kut kut kut kut quaa quaa quaa kut kut.* It came from above them.

Ernie looked up into a big tree. A gray squirrel stared right back at her. "Look!" Ernie pointed. But the squirrel zipped around to the other side of the tree. Ernie watched the spot. The squirrel peeked around the tree trunk. "There!" Ernie shouted.

Kut kut kut kut kut! answered the squirrel.

"What a welcoming committee," said Mommy.

"I'll say," said Daddy. He dropped his backpack on the ground. "Let's set up camp. Then we can see who else is in town."

They pitched three tents and unrolled

their sleeping bags inside them. Ernie and R.T. were in one tent. Michael and William were in the second. Mommy and Daddy were in the third. The squirrel chattered at them the whole time.

"We're probably covering up his hiding places," said Mommy.

"No wonder he is angry," said R.T. "We should leave some nuts out for him."

Next they dug a fire pit. Then they hiked through the woods to a stream. They brought back stones to put around their fire pit. Then everyone helped gather wood. Daddy brushed the dead leaves far away from the fire pit and laid a fire.

"This is hungry work," he said.

"No supper without water," said Mommy. So they all marched back to the farmhouse to get water from the pump.

On their way back through the cornfield, the sun began to set. The sky turned red and orange. The corn stubble shone. It was strangely silent. There were no street sounds.

No people sounds.

The blue jay had disappeared. Now there were other birds in the air, swooping and diving.

"Wow!" said Michael. "Just like Jupiter. Those birds are mini-pterodactyls."

"Quit saying that stuff, Michael," said William. "This is Earth."

R.T. shivered. "Look!" She pointed back at the farmhouse.

All they could see from the field was the falling-apart half. It glowed in the sunset like a burning coal.

Suddenly a great black bird lifted from the chimney. It flew straight up into the sky. It went up and up and up, as if it would fly all the way to the sun. Then it arced back down and disappeared among the other birds.

"Brrrr," said William. "I think it's getting cold." And they all walked a little faster back to the campsite.

CHAPTER 3

The Ghost of Little Eagle

Daddy lit the campfire right away. Mommy began to chop up vegetables. Soon the campsite felt as cozy as a kitchen.

While the fire burned merrily, everyone made supper packages. They each wrapped hamburger meat and potato slices and carrot sticks together in a piece of foil. When the fire burned down, they put their foil packages in the hot coals. Then they sang songs and waited.

The good smells started long before supper was ready. Ernie's stomach growled. She heard Michael's stomach rumble, too. Then R.T.'s. Then William's.

Ernie giggled. "Our tummies are louder than our singing," she said. By then the food was ready.

After supper, Daddy built up the fire again. They all sat around it, toasting marshmallows.

Ernie liked her marshmallows toasty brown. She was careful to keep them out of the fire. It took longer to toast them that way, but they tasted better.

William and R.T. cooked their marshmallows like Ernie. But Michael stuck his right into the flames. His marshmallow caught fire. When he blew it out, it was black.

"Mmmmm," said Michael. "Just right." Ernie wondered if he meant it.

"There sure are a lot more stars here than at home," said William.

"Not more," said Daddy. "You just see them better because there aren't any lights."

"Are those lights from a city?" asked

Michael. He pointed at a fuzzy whitish stripe across the sky.

"Nope," said Daddy. "That's the Milky Way. In the old days, people believed in a lot of gods. They thought the Milky Way was the road to the palace of heaven. Jupiter lived at the end of the road. He was the king of the gods. Other gods had palaces along the way."

Daddy pointed at a bright star in the sky. "That's the North Star," he told them. "Follow it down four stars, then over one, then up one, and you have the Little Dipper."

Ernie stared at the night sky. Those stars really did look like a dipper. A soup dipper dipping into star soup.

"How about those two over there?" asked William. He pointed at two bright stars.

"Castor and Pollux," said Daddy. "The story goes that Castor and Pollux were twins. They loved each other very much, and they were always together. Then Castor was killed in a war. Pollux begged Jupiter to let him die instead. Jupiter was amazed. He turned them both into stars so they could stay together."

"That's a nice story," said Michael. "But I think I'd like a ghost story next."

"A ghost story!" said Daddy. He pretended to shiver. "Are you *sure*?"

"*Yes!*" shouted Michael and William and R.T. and Ernie. "Tell us a ghost story!"

Daddy scratched his head. "Well now," he said. "Let me think. . . . Yes, I think I know one. Just let me get comfortable here."

He pulled a big log over to the fire and sat down on it. He leaned forward. He put his elbows on his knees and rubbed his hands together.

"Now then," he said. "This is another kind of star story. A ghost star story. Is everybody ready?"

"*Yes!*" shouted Michael and William and R.T. and Ernie again.

"Then, shhhhhhh," said Daddy. He looked around him.

Ernie looked around her, too. Were animals watching them from behind trees? Ernie shivered.

Then Daddy lowered his voice and began. "Once, on the very land where we are camping, there was another camp. An Ojibway camp. And in that camp, there was a young brave. Little Eagle was his name, for the eagle is the greatest bird in the sky, and the people knew that Little Eagle would someday be a great chief.

"Little Eagle could run with the deer. He could kill a buck with a single arrow. He could slip through the forest as quietly as a butterfly.

"Of course, many an Ojibway maiden hoped that Little Eagle would choose her to be his bride. But Little Eagle longed for something else. He didn't know what it was. Perhaps Mother Moon would show him.

He began to sleep outside under the stars, but he didn't sleep much. He was waiting for a sign.

"And then, one night, it came. A shooting star fell from the sky. It seemed to land in the center of the forest. Little Eagle arose and went to find it. Deeper and deeper into the forest he walked. He heard a trickle of water. Ahead he saw a soft, glowing light."

Ernie was holding her breath. She glanced at R.T. and William and Michael. Their faces glowed in the firelight. Michael had unpinned his space star. He was polishing it on his shirttail.

"Little Eagle crept silently toward the light. There, at the edge of a stream, he found—not a star, but a star maiden. Her black hair gleamed in the moonlight. Her soft skin glowed.

"Little Eagle was amazed. *She* was what was missing from his life! He had been waiting for the star maiden. And Mother Moon had known it.

"All night long, Little Eagle hid behind a tree. He watched the star maiden dance by the stream. Then at dawn, she disappeared. One minute she was there, the next she was gone. And Little Eagle hadn't yet said one word to her. He hung his head and returned to his village.

"They say that Little Eagle was never the same after that night. He wouldn't eat. He didn't seem to care about anything. Every night at dusk, he disappeared into the woods. In the mornings, he returned to the village sadder than ever. He never spoke a word about his sorrow, but sometimes people heard him moaning in his sleep.

"And then one night, Little Eagle went into the woods and did not return. His people grew worried. They sent search parties to find him. But no one ever did. Little Eagle had disappeared.

"Some people believe that he found his star maiden at last. This time, he spoke to her. And in the morning, she took him home with her, back to the sky.

"But others say that the ghost of Little Eagle is wandering still. Up and down the stream. Behind every tree. Under every thorny bush. Searching forever for his star maiden. And when the trees groan at night, don't think it's the wind. It's the ghost of Little Eagle moaning in his sleep."

CHAPTER 4

The Star Thief

"Romp and stomp! It's daylight in the swamp! I want to hear the pitter-patter of little feet on the forest floor!" Daddy yelled.

Ernie woke up. How could she help it after that?

The campsite was already bustling. *Kut kut kut kut.* The gray squirrel chased up and down his tree. *Sizzle sizzle spat.* Bacon and eggs cooked over the fire. *Slurp slurp slurp.* Daddy drank his coffee. *Caw caw caw.* The blue jay watched everything from his bush.

What a friendly morning, Ernie thought.

Soon they were all sitting around the campfire.

26

"Eggs taste better in the woods," said William.

"So does cocoa," said R.T.

"Everything is better in the woods," said Ernie.

Suddenly Michael jumped up. His eggs went flying. His cocoa spilled over the ground.

"It's gone!" he shouted.

"What's gone?" everyone else asked.

"My space star!" Michael yelled. He pulled at his collar. "It's gone!"

Sure enough, there was no star on Michael's collar.

"You must have taken it off," said R.T. "It's probably in your tent."

Michael raced into his tent. R.T. and William and Ernie raced after him. They searched the floor. They emptied the backpacks. They even shook out the sleeping bags. There was no star.

"Wait a minute," said Ernie. "Remember last night? Daddy was telling us about Little

Eagle. And you were polishing your star, Michael. I saw you. You must have dropped it. Your space star must be somewhere around the campfire."

"Eagle-Eye Ernie sees everything!" shouted William.

They all ran back outside. They searched all around the campfire. Mommy and Daddy helped. Daddy even poked around in the ashes. But there was no star.

"Look for tracks," said Ernie.

They found Ernie tracks and R.T. tracks. They found Michael and William tracks. They found Mommy and Daddy tracks. They even found squirrel tracks.

"Maybe the squirrel took it," said Ernie.

"To get back at us," said R.T., "for covering up his hiding places."

"It will turn up, Michael," said Mommy. "We'll keep looking."

But Michael was standing very still. "We won't find it," he whispered.

"What do you mean?" said Ernie. "Of

course we will find it. We are smarter than that old squirrel."

Michael shook his head. "The squirrel didn't take it," he said. "Little Eagle took it. Last night when we were all asleep. He thought it was his star maiden."

"Little Eagle is in the sky, Michael," said R.T. "With the star maiden."

"Only some people believe that," said Michael. "Other people believe he is still looking. I am one of *those* people."

"Then where are the moccasin tracks?" said William. "Little Eagle would be wearing moccasins." He was rubbing his lucky rabbit again. Ernie wished he would quit it. It was making her nervous.

"Ghosts don't leave tracks," said Michael.

"Oh, Michael," said Ernie. "Little Eagle was just a story. Daddy made it up. Didn't you, Daddy?"

Daddy nodded. "That's right, Michael," he said. "I did make it up. Honest."

Michael shook his head again. "You just

think you made it up. Ghosts can make you say strange things. They can get inside your head, and you never even know it."

William rubbed his lucky rabbit harder. "I *knew* something would go wrong," he said. He shivered. "It's getting colder, too."

Caw caw caw caw. The blue jay was still sitting on his bush, and he was still noisy. *Kut kut kut kut kut.* The squirrel was still chattering. Everyone else was silent. Ernie's friendly morning didn't seem so friendly anymore.

CHAPTER 5

Ghost Woods

"There's no sense moping around all day," said Daddy after lunch. "Let's go see if we can meet some of our neighbors."

"What neighbors?" asked William.

"I thought we were *alone* out here," said Michael. "Except for Little Eagle, I mean."

"You're never alone in the woods," said Daddy. "All around you, creatures are busy with their lives."

Caw caw caw caw. "Like that silly blue jay," said Ernie. "Except he's not busy with *his* life. He's just busy watching *our* lives."

Kut kut kut kut kut. "Or that squirrel," said R.T. "He's busy stealing space stars."

"I told you, he didn't steal it," said Michael. "Little Eagle stole it."

"Who else is in the woods?" asked William.

"Raccoons maybe," said Daddy. "Or rabbits or mice or foxes or snakes or deer."

"Or skunks?" asked Michael.

"Could be," said Daddy.

"Good," said Michael. "I'll get that old skunk to spray Little Eagle right in the face. That'll teach him not to steal stars from space commanders."

"You'll have to find that old skunk first," said Daddy. "And that may not be so easy. If the animals hear us coming, or smell us even, they will hide. We'll have to go like spies into those woods."

"We'll be spies!" Ernie shouted.

"Yeah," Michael agreed. "I'm the best space spy. Woods spying should be easy. I'll look for clues. I'll prove that Little Eagle stole my star."

"All right, then," said Daddy. "Let's go."

They followed a path into the woods. Ernie tried to step very softly, like a spy. She tried not to brush against any bushes. She tried to see everything. She tried to hear everything, too. She was trying so hard, she almost bumped into Daddy when he stopped.

"Look down here," he said. He pointed to a little path off the path they were on.

"We can't crawl through there," said Michael. "It's too low."

"*We* can't go there easily," said Daddy, "but a fox could. Or a raccoon. Or a skunk."

"Or a ghost," Michael added.

"Look at this," said Daddy. He pointed to a young tree. Some of its bark was gnawed away. "A porcupine could have done this, or maybe a rabbit."

"Not this, though," said Michael. He pointed to a smooth bare spot on a larger tree. "It's too high up. Porcupines and rabbits are too short to do this. Little Eagle must have done it. He used the bark to make a canoe."

Daddy smiled. "Why would a ghost need a canoe, Michael?" He shook his head. "No, I think a deer probably did that."

"I don't think so, Mr. Jones," said Michael. "I think Little Eagle wanted to take the star maiden for a canoe ride. That's why he needed a canoe."

Hooooooo . . . Shhhhhhh . . .

Ernie jumped. "What was that?"

"What was what?" asked R.T.

"Listen," said Ernie.

Everyone stopped and stood very still. Everyone listened. At first no one heard anything. Then, *Hooooooo . . . Shhhhhhh . . .* The sound came again.

"It's just the wind," said Daddy.

"Don't think it's the wind, Mr. Jones," said Michael. "It's Little Eagle moaning in his sleep."

"Oh, Michael," said R.T. "It's the middle of the day. No one is sleeping."

"Little Eagle is," said Michael. "He searches all night for his star maiden, so he has to sleep in the daytime. Besides, by now he knows my space star isn't his maiden. That would make him moan for sure."

Hooooooo . . . Shhhhhhh . . .

Ernie's tummy flip-flopped.

R.T. put her hands on her hips. "Just stop it, Michael," she said. "I don't want to hear about Little Eagle anymore. The squirrel took your star, and that's that!"

"Yeah," said William. He held on to his lucky rabbit. "The squirrel took it."

Ernie didn't say anything. Her tummy flip-flopped again. She wished it would stop it. She didn't even believe in ghosts. At least, she thought she didn't.

They hiked through the woods till they came to a stream.

"Is this the same stream we were at yesterday?" Ernie asked. Daddy nodded. "It looks bigger," said Ernie.

"It is," said Daddy. "We've come down-stream. And look at this." He pointed to a tree that was gnawed all the way through. "Little Eagle didn't do this, Michael. A beaver did it."

Smack!

Everyone jumped at the same time.

Ernie's tummy flip-flopped three times in a row.

"What was *that*?" William whispered.

"Little Eagle," whispered Michael.

"A beaver slapping his tail on the water," said Daddy.

Everyone looked at the stream.

"I don't see any beaver," William whispered.

"Me neither," said Michael and R.T. and Ernie.

"He's under the water now," Daddy explained. "If we keep walking by this stream, I bet we'll come to a beaver dam."

"No way!" said Michael. "These woods

are spooky. These are ghost woods. I'm going back."

Daddy laughed. "I thought you wanted to find Little Eagle's ghost," he said.

"I'll find him tomorrow," said Michael. "Right now I'm another kind of spy—a supper spy!"

They headed back to the campsite. They all made a lot of noise along the way. Ernie's tummy stopped flip-flopping.

"Supper, supper, supper spies," she began to chant.

"Supper spies will get the prize," said Daddy.

"We are super supper spies," added Ernie.

"Because we know where supper lies," Daddy finished.

Then everyone began to chant. They chanted and marched all the way back.

"You sounded like a herd of elephants tromping through the woods," said Mommy. "I could hear you a mile away."

"What's for supper?" shouted Michael.

"Campfire chili," Mommy shouted back and laughed. "It will be ready in half an hour."

"Hooray!" shouted Michael and R.T. and William and Daddy. But Ernie didn't shout. Half an hour was just what she needed. Half an hour to think. She slipped away and walked up the path to the cornfield. No one would bother her there. R.T. and William and Michael all felt spooky about the cornfield.

Ernie sat down under a cornstalk. She didn't feel spooky. A cornfield was just a cornfield. A sunset was just a sunset. "There's no such thing as ghosts," she told herself right out loud. Only Michael believed that Little Eagle stole his star. And maybe William. R.T. didn't believe it. She thought the squirrel stole it.

Was it the squirrel? Ernie wondered. She liked that idea better than the one about it being a ghost. But why would a squirrel take a gold star? Gold stars didn't look anything at all like nuts.

Whisker whisker whisker.

What was *that*? Ernie froze. Her tummy flip-flopped so much it almost turned upside down. Her heart pounded.

Whisker whisker whisker.

There it was again. Ernie looked around her very carefully. She turned her head very slowly. She didn't move the rest of her body at all.

Then she saw it! A little mouse was scurrying off between the cornstalks. Ernie knew he had been taking corn.

Ernie held her breath. She sat very still. She watched until the little mouse disappeared. Then she let her breath out. Her heart leaped inside her. She had seen her first wild animal. She was a true woods spy now. Or at least a cornstalk spy. *And* she had a new suspect. The thief could be a mouse.

Gold stars looked more like corn than nuts did, after all.

The star thief wasn't any ghost! Even if it wasn't a mouse, Ernie felt sure now that it was some kind of animal. Not a deer or a fox, probably. But raccoons and beavers had paws shaped like little hands. They could steal gold stars, maybe.

Caw caw caw caw caw caw caw!

Ernie looked up. That noisy blue jay was sitting on a cornstalk right above her. What was he doing here anyway? He belonged back on his bush. That's where he always seemed to be.

Jay jay jay jay jay caw caw caw caw!

How could she think with all that racket? That bird would drive her nuts!

Oh, well. Supper was probably ready by now anyway. Ernie got up and started back to the campsite. She felt very pleased with herself. And her tummy, finally, felt very quiet.

CHAPTER 6

The Ghost of Trapper Jack

There were s'mores for dessert that night—toasted marshmallows and chocolate sandwiched between two graham crackers. The stars were just as bright as last night. Michael still burned his marshmallows. And he still wanted ghost stories, too. Ernie was surprised. He must have gotten brave again since the afternoon.

"I don't know, Michael," said Daddy. "One ghost seems to be all we can handle. I don't want you to get *too* scared."

"Ghosts don't scare me," said Michael. "Come on, Mr. Jones. Your stories are the greatest. Tell us another one. *Please?*"

"Yeah!" "Please!" "Come on!" said the others. "We won't get scared!"

They all must have gotten brave again. It was the campfire that did it, Ernie thought. It was so cozy.

"Well, I guess one more won't hurt," said Daddy.

The fire crackled. Daddy stretched his legs toward it. He leaned back against a log. Then he began. "Long ago, Minnesota was wilderness. The Dakota people lived here. And the Ojibway people . . ."

"Like Little Eagle," said Michael.

"Yes," said Daddy, "like Little Eagle. Then the explorers came. They saw the great Mississippi River. They saw the thick forests. They saw the good earth. Soon others were moving to Minnesota. Farmers. Soldiers. Trappers. And one of those trappers was a bad man named Jack. . . ."

"Trappers are mean," said R.T. "They kill the animals to make fur coats and stuff."

"But some are meaner than others," said Daddy. "And Jack was the meanest of the lot. The more animals he killed, the happier Jack was. You see, Jack was a very greedy man. All he wanted was to get rich.

"And he did get rich. He killed many, many animals. Then he sold their skins. He bought jewels. Diamonds. Rubies. Amethysts. He kept them all in a box. Every night, he opened his box. He ran his fingers through all his jewels, and he laughed with greedy glee.

"And every night, the animals heard Jack laughing. How they hated that sound!

"But the killing just went on and on. Otters and raccoons. Beavers and foxes. Would it never end? Finally, the animals had had enough. A great meeting was held in the forest, and the animals thought of a plan to drive Jack away.

"From then on, Jack never got a full night's sleep. The animals kept him awake. Bears surrounded his cabin. Coyotes howled through the night. Skunks sprayed him. Raccoons raided his food supplies.

"Finally Jack could stand it no longer. He leaped from his bed. He ran out his door and into the forest.

"But by then Jack was almost out of his mind. He forgot where he had laid his traps. And sure enough, he stepped right into one. Jack had trapped himself!"

"Hooray!" shouted R.T.

"What happened then?" asked William. He was squeezing his lucky rabbit.

"Jack called for help," said Daddy, "but no one heard him. Not even the animals. For they were making their own noise. You see, they had discovered Jack's jewels.

"Oh, what a wailing began then. The animals could not bear it. Those worthless stones were all they had of their lost friends. And so they did the only thing they knew how to do. They carried the stones back into the forest. They scattered the jewels through the woods."

"What happened to Jack?" asked William.

"No one knows," said Daddy. "But they say, on moonlit nights, you can hear his ghost. He wanders through the forest, dragging the trap behind him, searching for his jewels. But he will never find them."

"Why not?" whispered William.

"An amazing thing happened to those jewels," said Daddy. "Time passed. Peace returned to the forest. And the jewels began to change. The diamonds turned into dewdrops. The rubies turned into berries. And the amethysts turned into lady's slippers. They say the spirits of all those animals came home."

William sighed and let go of his rabbit. "That's sad," he said.

"Diamonds into dewdrops," said R.T. "I like that. Maybe my ring . . ." She looked at her hand. *"My ring!"* she shouted. *"It's gone!"*

CHAPTER 7

The Masked Bandit

Ernie and R.T. whispered far into the night. And the forest whispered, too. *Hooooooooo . . . Shhhhhhhhh . . .*

"It's Little Eagle," whispered R.T. Her voice shook.

"You don't believe in ghosts," Ernie whispered back. "You said the squirrel stole Michael's star."

"Maybe I was wrong," R.T. whispered. "Why would a squirrel want a gold star, anyway? Maybe Michael was right. Maybe Little Eagle did take his star. And maybe Trapper Jack took my diamond ring. Maybe these woods are full of ghosts."

"There's no such thing as ghosts," Ernie whispered.

"How do you know?" R.T. whispered back. "Just listen a minute."

Ernie stopped whispering and listened. The wind whistled through the trees. Branches creaked and moaned and sighed. The leaves on the ground rustled in the darkness. A twig snapped.

"Ghosts," whispered R.T. "Little Eagle. Trapper Jack. Who knows how many more? Can't you hear them all walking through the woods?"

"That's just the wind," Ernie whispered back.

Plunk-clatter-tin-tin-tin.

Ernie jumped inside her sleeping bag.

"*That* wasn't any wind," R.T. whispered. "That was Trapper Jack dragging his trap behind him."

Ernie shivered. She curled up tight inside her sleeping bag. She *didn't* believe in ghosts. She *didn't* believe in Trapper Jack.

There had to be some other explanation.

"It's the wind blowing a pot around," she whispered.

R.T. didn't say anything.

"Listen, R.T.," said Ernie. "I saw a mouse taking corn from a cornstalk this afternoon. Some animal took Michael's star. And some animal took your ring, too."

"Animals take food," whispered R.T. "They don't take stars and rings."

Ernie didn't know what to say. She *didn't* believe in ghosts, no matter what R.T. and Michael said. An animal *must* have taken those things. But how could she ever prove it? She would have to find the animal's hiding place. And that would not be easy.

The moonlight shone into the tent. It made shadows on the walls. It made R.T.'s hair look silver. It made her face look white.

Ernie tried one more time. "There are no such things as ghosts," she whispered.

But R.T. didn't answer.

The wind whistled around the tent. The

branches moaned and groaned. Unseen creatures scurried through the night. Ernie inched her sleeping bag closer to R.T.'s. Finally she fell asleep.

CRASH! CLANG! BANG! *"Shoo!"* *"Scat, you varmint!"* *"AM-scray!"*

Waking up in the woods was sure noisy, Ernie thought.

She hopped out of her sleeping bag. She ran to the tent door. R.T. was already there.

"What's going on?" asked Ernie.

"Just look!" said R.T.

Ernie looked outside. What a mess! There was garbage everywhere. Orange peels. Banana peels. Half a peanut butter sandwich. Tin foil. The trail mix Michael had spilled. Everything they had eaten yesterday. And everything it was wrapped in, too. Even the garbage bag was all torn up.

And right in the middle of it all was a fat raccoon. He was holding an orange peel. He didn't look scared at all.

Mommy and Daddy banged on pots and pans. *"Shoo!"* they shouted. "Go home!"

Even the blue jay was scolding that raccoon. *Caw caw caw caw caw.* The blue jay was guarding his bush. What was so special about that bush anyway? Ernie wondered.

The raccoon looked at them all through his black mask. Then he slowly turned around. He waddled down the path. He didn't hurry at all. He looked back over his shoulder. That raccoon looked sorry to be leaving! Then he disappeared into the woods.

Mommy and Daddy began to clean up the mess.

"It's all my fault," said Mommy. "I forgot to take our garbage to the house last night."

"I should never have told that Trapper Jack story," said Daddy. "It spooked all of us."

"All of us *except* that raccoon!" said Mommy. She started to laugh. "Did you see the look on his face?" She laughed harder.

54

Daddy was laughing, too.

By then Ernie and R.T. and William and Michael were all laughing, too.

"You sure looked funny, Mr. Jones!" said Michael.

Caw caw caw caw caw caw caw caw!

"You sure did, Mr. Jones," said Mommy. "Even Mr. Jay thinks so." She held her sides and laughed harder.

"You looked pretty silly yourself, Mrs. Jones," said Daddy.

"I bet I did," said Mommy. She sat down on a log. She grinned at Ernie and R.T. and William and Michael. "Well, don't just stand there, campers," she said. "Get dressed. Then give us a hand."

Mommy started making breakfast. Everyone else helped pick up garbage.

Caw caw caw caw jay jay jay! The blue jay hopped from bush to bush, watching them.

"I guess he thinks we're pretty dumb," said Daddy.

"He's right," said Mommy.

Ernie watched the blue jay. He *did* look as if he thought they were dumb. He looked as if he was scolding them now. But why? Ernie wondered. Why was he always *here*, anyway? Why was he sitting on that bush making noise all the time? It was as if he was guarding something. But why would he be guarding a bush in November?

By then the campsite was cleaned up. Breakfast was ready. They all sat down to eat.

"At least the mystery is solved," said Daddy.

"What do you mean?" asked William.

"The ring and the star," said Daddy. "That raccoon seems to know this campsite pretty well. He has been here before. He is your masked bandit, I bet."

Michael shook his head. "I still think it was Little Eagle," he said. "A raccoon wouldn't want a space star."

"He's right," said R.T. "He wouldn't

want a diamond ring, either. All raccoons want is something to eat."

"Didn't you see him holding that orange peel?" said William. "Gold stars look sort of orange. Maybe he thought it was food."

"Raccoons aren't that dumb," said R.T. "He would have smelled that it wasn't food."

"Yeah," said Michael. "Little Eagle stole my star."

"And Trapper Jack stole my ring," said R.T. "I even heard him last night. He was dragging his trap behind him. He must have been looking for more stuff to steal."

William rubbed his lucky rabbit. "I think Mr. Jones is right," he said.

"Little Eagle!" shouted Michael.

"Trapper Jack!" shouted R.T.

"Raccoon!" shouted William.

But Ernie didn't say a word. A new idea was stirring in her mind. A silly idea. A wonderful idea. An idea that would surprise them all.

Michael and R.T. and William were still arguing, but Ernie wasn't listening anymore. She was too busy watching the blue jay.

He had left his bush. Now he was on the ground. Ernie saw a piece of foil they had missed. The blue jay hopped over to it. He poked it. He pecked it. He pushed it around. He pecked a piece of it right off. Then he picked it up in his beak. He hopped back over to his bush. He disappeared beneath it. When he came out, the foil was gone.

Ernie had been right! The thief *was* an animal. Just not the animal William and Daddy thought it was. This animal had stolen those things right in front of their eyes. He had made a lot of noise about it, too. And they had never once suspected him.

Her eagle eye had done it again! But Ernie didn't say anything yet. She just smiled. She was hatching a plan. A trick that no one would ever forget.

CHAPTER 8

Prizes and Surprises

Mommy was hike leader today.

"We're going hunting," she told them.

"Hunting!" said R.T. "Like Trapper Jack? I won't go!"

"No, silly," said Michael. *"For* Trapper Jack, and for Little Eagle."

"For the raccoon," said William, "and for the star and the ring."

Mommy laughed. "You're all wrong," she said. She handed them each a list:

1 mushroom
1 perfect red leaf
1 animal track
1 hole in a tree
1 bug
1 smooth stone
1 rotting log
1 yellow leaf
1 fern
1 patch of moss
1 beehive
1 bird's nest

"The hunt is for these," said Mommy.

Michael groaned. "I don't want to hunt for this stuff. I want to hunt for the thief."

"You mean, the thieves," said R.T.

"The first one to find everything on the list will win a prize," said Mommy.

"What kind of prize?" said Michael. "A gold space star?"

"A diamond ring?" said R.T.

"I'm afraid not," said Mommy. "But

something you will like. Something for campers. Are you ready?"

"Ready!" shouted Michael. "I can look for this stuff and Little Eagle at the same time."

"Ready!" shouted R.T. "I can look for Trapper Jack at the same time, too."

"Ready!" shouted William. He rubbed his rabbit for luck.

"What about you, Ernie?" Mommy asked.

"I'm not going," said Ernie. "I want to help Daddy cook the turkey. All right?"

"Well, I guess so," said Mommy. "Anyone else want to stay?"

Ernie held her breath. She crossed her fingers behind her back. If anyone else stayed, her plan would be ruined.

"No way!" shouted Michael. "Cooking is bor-ing!"

"I'm going hunting!" shouted R.T.

"Me too!" shouted William.

Ernie uncrossed her fingers. She let out her breath.

The hunters started down the path.

Ernie waved. "Bye!" she called after them. "Good luck!" Then they disappeared. Ernie smiled. She and Daddy were alone. Alone with the blue jay.

Daddy had made a cooking spit. He stuck it through the turkey. Then he hung the spit on two forked sticks. The turkey was in the middle, right over the fire.

"I didn't know you were interested in cooking, Ernie," said Daddy.

"I'm not," said Ernie. "I'm interested in blue jays."

"Huh?" said Daddy.

"Just watch," said Ernie.

Ernie walked over to the blue jay's bush. She got down on her hands and knees. She crawled under the bush.

When she came out, her hands made fists. She held them out to Daddy.

"Pick one," she said.

Daddy picked the left fist. Ernie opened her hand. The diamond ring sparkled in her palm.

"Now pick the other," said Ernie.

"I don't believe this!" said Daddy. He picked the right fist. Ernie opened it. There was the gold space star!

"How on earth . . ." said Daddy.

"It was the blue jay!" said Ernie. "Caw caw caw caw caw!" she shouted. She hopped around like a bird.

Daddy laughed. "But how did you figure it out, Ernie?" he asked.

Ernie told him about the foil.

Caw caw caw caw caw caw caw caw caw!

"Here he is again," said Daddy. "I hope he doesn't remember what he stole."

Ernie tucked the ring and the star into her pocket. "For safekeeping," she said.

Daddy rubbed her head. "It's that eagle eye of yours, Ernie. You are the best detective I know. We should all have suspected that blue jay from the start."

"Why?" asked Ernie.

"Blue jays are like crows," said Daddy. "They like shiny things. I've heard stories about them stealing pennies and bottle caps. I guess I just forgot."

"And now I have another plan," said Ernie. She whispered into Daddy's ear.

Daddy laughed and laughed. "We'd better get cooking, then," he told her.

Ernie and Daddy cooked sweet potatoes in foil at the edge of the fire. They cooked carrots and onions the same way. They kept turning the turkey so it would get brown all over.

Finally it was time to make dessert: Indian Pudding. Ernie mixed some cornmeal with some cold water. Daddy boiled some more water with a little salt. Then they mixed everything together. They stirred and stirred it so it wouldn't get lumpy. It got thicker and thicker.

"Looks done to me," said Daddy. He added some sugar and stirred it in.

Ernie washed the star and the ring. Then she dropped them into the pudding. She stirred them in. Then she put the pudding on a large stone next to the fire. That way it would stay warm. She put a cover on the pudding pot. That way the pudding would keep its secrets.

CHAPTER 9

The Three Wishes

"I won!" shouted William. "I found everything on the list!"

Ernie bet she knew why. William hadn't been looking for ghosts, too. Michael and R.T. had.

"Congratulations, William," said Daddy.

Michael kicked a stone. "We didn't find Little Eagle, though," he said.

"Or Trapper Jack, either," said R.T.

"Or the raccoon," said William. "Or the star. Or the ring."

"We'll never get them back now," said R.T.

"I don't think Julia has another star," said Michael.

They sounded so sad that Ernie almost gave away her secret. But she didn't.

"I think it's time for prizes," said Mommy.

"Prizes?" asked Michael. "I thought only William got a prize."

"Surprise, Michael," said Mommy. She handed him a paper bag. She gave one to R.T. and Ernie, too. William got two.

Michael opened his bag. He pulled out his prize.

"A tuna fish can?" he said.

Mommy laughed. She took the can and pulled it open. It turned into a cup. Then she squashed it shut again.

"Wow!" said Michael. "A space cup is almost as good as a space star."

"They are camping cups," said Mommy. "For camping on Earth or in space. One for each of you, because you have all been such terrific campers."

Then William opened his second bag. Inside was a hat. A camping hat.

"It's a camouflage hat," Mommy explained. "So the animals won't notice you in the woods."

William put on the hat right away. "I'll let you wear it when you camp on Jupiter," he told Michael. "Thank you, Mrs. Jones."

"You're welcome, William." She sniffed the air. "It smells like you two have been busy," she told Ernie and Daddy.

Daddy winked at Ernie. "Busier than you think," he said. "Step right up for the best Thanksgiving dinner you'll ever have."

He was right. The fire crackled. The air was filled with the good smells of burning wood and roasted turkey. Over their heads was the blue November sky. And the food was delicious.

Michael chewed on a drumstick. "How about a Thanksgiving ghost story, Mr. Jones?" he asked.

"No way, Michael!" said Daddy. "My

ghost story days are over. Every time I tell one, something disappears."

"That's true," said R.T. "You must have special powers, Mr. Jones."

"Ghost powers," said Michael.

Then William found the wishbone. He tucked it into his pocket. "I'm going to save it," he said.

"Why?" asked Ernie.

"I have too many wishes," William explained.

"Like what?" asked R.T.

"Like, Number One, I wish we would find your ring," said William. "And Number Two, I wish we would find Michael's space star."

Ernie jumped to her feet. "Time for dessert!" she shouted.

She dished up six bowls of Indian Pudding. Then she sat down and waited.

Michael put his spoon into his pudding. He stirred it around.

"There's a rock in mine," he said.

"Mine too," said R.T.

They lifted their spoons.

"It's my ring!" R.T. shouted.

"And my space star!" shouted Michael.

"How on earth . . ." said Mommy.

"I never got a wish so fast before," said William. "Two wishes."

Then, of course, Ernie had to explain everything.

"Well, I never!" said Mommy when Ernie was finished.

"Three cheers for Eagle Eye!" shouted Michael. "Hip, hip—"

"Hooray!"

"Hip, hip—"

"Hooray!"

"Hip, hip—"

"HOORAY!"

William took the wishbone out of his pocket. "I can make my wish now," he told them. "I only have one left."

He held the wishbone out to Ernie.

"I wish we could go camping every year!" he shouted.

Then they pulled.

William got the short end, but Ernie was certain he would get his wish anyway. She had wished for exactly the same thing!

BUY ONE **EAGLE-EYE ERNIE**™ MYSTERY AND RECEIVE ONE FREE!

The adventures continue... but not the cost!

Regulations:

1. All coupons must include proof of EAGLE-EYE ERNIE purchase.
2. Limit one free book per household.
3. Offer expires May 31, 1991
4. Entries must be legible. Not responsible for lost or misdirected mail.
5. Simon & Schuster employees and their families are not eligible.